The Mystery of the White Elephant

THREE COUSINS DETECTIVE CLUB®

#1 / The Mystery of the White Elephant
#2 / The Mystery of the Silent Nightingale
#3 / The Mystery of the Wrong Dog
#4 / The Mystery of the Dancing Angels
#5 / The Mystery of the Hobo's Message
#6 / The Mystery of the Magi's Treasure
#7 / The Mystery of the Haunted Lighthouse
#8 / The Mystery of the Dolphin Detective
#9 / The Mystery of the Eagle Feather
#10 / The Mystery of the Silly Goose
#11 / The Mystery of the Copycat Clown
#12 / The Mystery of the Honeybees' Secret
#13 / The Mystery of the Gingerbread House
#14 / The Mystery of the Zoo Camp
#15 / The Mystery of the Goldfish Pond
#16 / The Mystery of the Traveling Button
#17 / The Mystery of the Birthday Party
#18 / The Mystery of the Lost Island
#19 / The Mystery of the Wedding Cake
#20 / The Mystery of the Sand Castle
#21 / The Mystery of the Sock Monkeys
#22 / The Mystery of the African Gray
#23 / The Mystery of the Butterfly Garden
#24 / The Mystery of the Book Fair
#25 / The Mystery of the Coon Cat
#26 / The Mystery of the Runaway Scarecrow
#27 / The Mystery of the Attic Lion
#28 / The Mystery of the Backdoor Bundle
#29 / The Mystery of the Painted Snake
#30 / The Mystery of the Golden Reindeer

YOUNG COUSINS MYSTERIES®

#1 / The Birthday Present Mystery
#2 / The Sneaky Thief Mystery
#3 / The Giant Chicken Mystery
#4 / The Chalk Drawings Mystery
#5 / The Purple Cow Mystery
#6 / The Flying Pigs Mystery

www.elspethcampbellmurphy.com

The Mystery of the White Elephant

Elspeth Campbell Murphy

Illustrated by Joe Nordstrom

BETHANY HOUSE PUBLISHERS
MINNEAPOLIS, MINNESOTA 55438

Published by Bethany House Publishers
11400 Hampshire Avenue South
Bloomington, Minnesota 55438
www.bethanyhouse.com

Bethany House Publishers is a Division of
Baker Book House Company, Grand Rapids, Michigan.

Printed in the United States of America

Library of Congress Cataloging-in-Publication Data

Murphy, Elspeth Campbell.
    The mystery of the white elephant / Elspeth Campbell Murphy.
        p.   cm. — (Three Cousins Detective Club® ; 1)
    Summary: When Timothy and his cousins go to the church swap
meet, they discover a thief has stolen the white elephant they plan to
buy, and it's up to them to find the culprit.
    [1. Mystery and detective stories. 2. Rummage sales—Fiction.
3. Cousins—Fiction. 4. Christian life—Fiction.] I. Title.
II. Series: Murphy, Elspeth Campbell. Three Cousins Detective
Club™ ; 1.
PZ7.M95316Myp   1994
[Fic]—dc20   94-16719
ISBN 1-55661-405-5   CIP
                                          AC

In loving memory of my father-in-law,

Howard R. Murphy,

whose life was filled with
love, joy, peace,
patience, kindness, goodness,
faithfulness, gentleness, and self-control.

ELSPETH CAMPBELL MURPHY has been a familiar name in Christian publishing for over fifteen years, with more than seventy-five books to her credit and sales reaching five million worldwide. She is the author of the best-selling series *David and I Talk to God* and *The Kids From Apple Street Church*, as well as the 1990 Gold Medallion winner *Do You See Me, God?* A graduate of Trinity College and Moody Bible Institute, Elspeth and her husband, Mike, make their home in Chicago, where she writes full time.

Contents

1

An Elephant in the Attic?

"Timothy, do me a favor," said his mother, all in a rush. "I have to finish baking these cookies for the church picnic. Take your cousins up to the attic and see if you can find a white elephant. We need to take it to the church picnic with us. Everyone is supposed to bring a white elephant."

Timothy Dawson looked across the kitchen table at his cousins Sarah-Jane Cooper and Titus McKay. They looked back at him. They all looked at Timothy's mother.

Had she really said what they thought she said?

"Ex*cuse* me?" said Timothy. "Did you just tell us to get a white elephant out of the attic?"

Timothy's mother looked up from what she was doing and laughed. "The term 'white elephant' is just a way of speaking. It means something you have that you don't like or need. Something that's more trouble than it's worth. It just gets in the way, but somehow you can't bring yourself to throw it out."

The cousins thought about this for a minute.

Sarah-Jane said, "So—this thing doesn't actually have to be like a china elephant or something?"

"That's right," said her Aunt Sarah. "A 'white elephant' is just what it's called."

"Why is it called that?" asked Titus.

Timothy's mother explained. "It comes from a story about a country that used to be called Siam. When the king of Siam had a proud and bossy person at court, he had a way to deal with him. The king would give that obnoxious person a very special present. A rare white elephant. A real one. Now, this *seemed* like a great honor. But actually it was a punishment. That's because a white elephant was

10

considered so special it couldn't be used for work. It just ate and ate and got in the way. The owner went broke just feeding it! But since it was a present from the king, the owner couldn't give it away. So he was stuck with a white elephant he didn't want or need."

Titus said, "It makes you feel sorry for the guy. I mean, I know he was obnoxious and everything, but still . . ."

"I feel sorry for the elephant!" declared Sarah-Jane. "I wouldn't want to be a white elephant and just get in the way."

Her aunt laughed. "That's something you don't have to worry about, Sarah-Jane. God doesn't have any white elephants. He doesn't want any of us to stand around thinking we're better than everybody else. And He doesn't want any of us to feel useless, either. He loves us so much He wants the best for us. That's why it's OK to call a *thing* a 'white elephant,' but not a person."

"One more question," said Timothy. "Why are we taking *this* white-elephant thing to church?"

"Each family has to bring something for the swap meet," replied his mother. "After the picnic, we'll have an auction to sell the white elephants. The money will go to the church building fund."

"Let me get this straight," said Titus. "We take something we want to get rid of—so someone can buy it. But then we have to buy something that someone else wants to get rid of?"

His aunt laughed. "That's about the size of it. Sounds crazy, I know. But we might actually find something we like at the swap meet. One person's white elephant is another person's treasure."

Sarah-Jane said, "What if we take something we like—and we don't see anything at the swap meet that we like better? Can we bid on our own elephant?"

Aunt Sarah shook her head. "No, that's one of the rules. No one in the family—or the family's guests—can go home with the same thing they brought. And I think you guys slipped in a couple of extra questions. So get to work!"

2

Perfectly Awful

*T*imothy had never been in his attic without a grown-up before. Sarah-Jane and Titus had never been in Timothy's attic at all.

But this morning Timothy's mother was super busy. Especially since she had stopped to answer so many questions about white elephants. And Timothy's father had taken Timothy's baby sister, Priscilla, grocery shopping with him. So it was up to Timothy—with the help of his cousins, of course—to find the family's white elephant.

Timothy divided the attic into three sections, and they each took one part. They set to

13

work, searching for the perfect white elephant. They didn't know exactly what they were searching for. But they knew they would know it when they found it. It couldn't be anything broken. And it couldn't be anything junky. And they knew that it didn't actually have to be an elephant.

"How about this, Tim?" Titus asked, sounding a little doubtful. He held up a clunky, boring lamp.

"It's very ugly, Tim," said Sarah-Jane, super politely, as if it were a compliment.

"Yes," said Timothy. "But it's just plain ugly. You know what I mean? We want something weirder. Something funnier. Let's keep looking."

So they kept looking.

And looking.

In a way, this was the perfect job for them. That's because searching is a big part of detective work. And the cousins were used to detective work. They even had a club for it called the Three Cousins Detective Club. In fact, they had solved a lot of mysteries. But even when they didn't have an actual mystery to solve, they liked to play detective games to keep in practice.

So they kept on looking and looking for the perfect white elephant to take to the church swap meet. And finally all that looking paid off.

Dusty, but grinning from ear to ear, Timothy pulled something out of the corner and held it up.

"Ti! S-J! I think I found it!"

Timothy unwrapped the clear plastic it was wrapped in. It was a mirror. It had a fancy frame all around it. The frame was covered with fake pearls and jewels and china flowers and chubby baby angels. One of the cherubs even had a bunch of grapes on his head.

Titus and Sarah-Jane just stared at it for a minute as if they couldn't think of a thing to say.

Finally Sarah-Jane said, "Where in the world did that come from?"

"I have no idea," said Timothy. "I never saw it before in my life. What do you think?"

"What do I think?" said Sarah-Jane. "I think it's *perfect*."

"Perfectly awful, you mean," said Titus, nodding his head with satisfaction.

Timothy agreed. "Perfectly, perfectly, perfectly awful. Lady and Gentleman, we have our white elephant."

3

Baby Elephant

The cousins agreed that they were each going to keep a straight face when they showed the mirror to Pastor Parry. They had come over to church early because they couldn't wait to put the perfectly awful mirror on display.

Pastor Parry kept a straight face, too. "Well, now, Timothy," he said. "That is a mirror. Yes. That certainly is a mirror."

But they couldn't keep it up. All four of them burst out laughing.

Timothy said, "I never saw it before. My dad said that's because it's been up in the attic since way before I was born. My parents got the mirror as a wedding present."

Sarah-Jane explained, "Aunt Sarah said it's nicely made. But it's much too glitzy for their house."

Titus said, "That's because it's the glitziest mirror in the whole history of the world."

"Could be," said Pastor Parry. "But probably someone will think it's just wonderful."

Timothy agreed. "My mom says one person's white elephant is another person's treasure."

"And she said only *things* can be white elephants. Not people," added Sarah-Jane. "Aunt Sarah says God doesn't have any white elephants."

"She's right," said Pastor Parry. "No matter how bad someone might look to us, God looks at that person and sees something to treasure."

Titus said, "If God came to a swap meet, and all the things were people, he would want all of them."

Pastor Parry laughed. "Exactly so. But I'm not sure I would want to take home all the things on *these* tables. As long as you're here early, you should look around for something

18

you'd like your family to bid on. We're starting to fill up the display tables, I see. It should be a great day. It's not a sunny day. But at least it looks as if the rain is going to hold off."

The cousins took Pastor Parry's advice and wandered around by the tables. They were searching again. But this time they were searching for a white elephant they'd like to buy. It was really up to Timothy's parents to decide what to bid on, of course. But the cousins thought it wouldn't hurt to give them some ideas. And even that was mostly up to Timothy.

They saw lots of lamps.

And lots of vases.

And lots and lots of knickknacks.

Sarah-Jane thought there were quite a few possibilities. But Timothy and Titus didn't see eye to eye with Sarah-Jane on the subject of knickknacks. Once, at a flea market, Sarah-Jane had bought a china cat that looked as if it were laughing. The boys had thought she was crazy at the time. But now they had to admit that the laughing cat had led to quite an adventure. And that was the start of their detective club.

Today, Timothy didn't see anything he liked. Until he spotted the baby elephant.

"Look, you guys!" he said to his cousins. "Somebody actually brought a white elephant to the white elephant sale!"

"EXcellent!" said Titus.

"So cool!" said Sarah-Jane.

The baby elephant was actually a china cookie jar. It was sitting up like a teddy bear. It wore a ruffly bonnet and held an ice cream cone in its trunk. It had such a funny little smile on its face that it made you want to smile right back.

4

Another Person's Treasure

A lady Timothy knew from church came up to them. Her name was Mrs. Foster. Mrs. Foster was wearing a funny little kind of smile herself—as if maybe she was embarrassed.

"What do you think of my white elephant?" she asked.

"It's neat-O!" said Timothy.

Mrs. Foster looked as if she couldn't quite believe her ears. "Really? Really, do you like it? You don't think it was a silly thing to bring?"

"No!" said Timothy. "My mom will love it. She likes to bake cookies."

"Well, I hope she gets it at the auction

then," said Mrs. Foster. "I've had that cookie jar for ages. But I never bake anything. It was just taking up room in the cupboard. I thought it would be funny to bring a white elephant to a white elephant sale."

"I think it's a great idea," said Timothy. "A white elephant that *really is* a white elephant!"

"Well, I'm glad to hear that," said Mrs. Foster. "Because my houseguest thought I was crazy. She even offered to buy the cookie jar herself for a few dollars so that I would bring something else and not be embarrassed."

Sarah-Jane asked, "Your friend won't mind if Aunt Sarah buys it, will she? Because I don't think guests can bid on what their friends brought."

"That's right, they can't," agreed Mrs. Foster. "But my friend isn't interested in the swap meet. And I didn't ask her to come early to help set up. She's been on vacation in Canada. And I think she's rather tired from the trip. But she said she'd walk over later for the picnic. She just offered to buy the elephant to be nice."

"Well, I don't think you should be embarrassed about it at all," said Titus.

"Your white elephant is the *only* thing I saw that I liked," said Timothy.

"There *are* some rather unusual things here," agreed Mrs. Foster. "Did you see that really fancy mirror? Do you know who brought that?"

The cousins glanced at one another—then stared at their shoes. Now who was embarrassed?

But before they could say anything, Mrs. Foster went on. "That's what *I* want to buy.

That mirror is the most beautiful thing I've ever seen!"

Could they have been wrong about the mirror?

After Mrs. Foster left them, the cousins went back to take another look at it.

Nope.

It was still as perfectly awful as ever.

They were just about to go see if Timothy's parents were there yet when Timothy froze.

"Don't turn around," he whispered to Titus and Sarah-Jane.

5

The Stranger in the Mirror

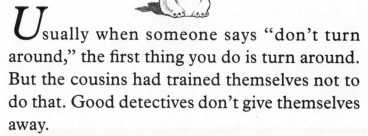

Usually when someone says "don't turn around," the first thing you do is turn around. But the cousins had trained themselves not to do that. Good detectives don't give themselves away.

"What is it?" murmured Titus.

Timothy said softly, "Look in the mirror. Pretend like you're interested in buying it. But use it to see what's going on behind you. Do you see anything strange?"

Very, *very* casually the cousins took turns looking in the mirror.

"I see a lady hanging around by that big

tree," said Titus. "She's got a beige tote bag with some kind of red leaf design in the corner of it. And she's wearing a rain poncho. Why would you wear a rain poncho when it looks like the rain is going to hold off?"

"And the sun hat," added Sarah-Jane. "Why would you wear a big, floppy hat on a cloudy day?"

Timothy said, "That's what I mean. Why would you wear a rain poncho and a sun hat *at the same time*. Especially when you don't need either one."

This was exactly the kind of detective game the cousins loved to play. They would notice what was going on around them and ask themselves questions about it. They especially noticed things that seemed somehow odd or out of place. Sometimes, of course, they actually stumbled onto a real mystery. Sometimes not. But the cousins' motto was: *Keep alert. Pay attention.*

As they watched, the lady moved away from the tree. They couldn't see her in the mirror anymore. But by turning a little bit, they could watch her out of the corner of their eyes.

She wandered casually up to the tables.

Pastor Parry glanced her way. He started over as if to say hello. But the lady didn't wait. Instead, she turned and hurried away. The cousins got a last glimpse of her as she slipped through the side door of the church.

The cousins glanced at one another. Should they keep up the detective game and follow her?

But at that moment Timothy's parents and baby sister found them.

Priscilla squealed with delight when she saw Timothy, Titus, and Sarah-Jane—even though she had seen them only a little while ago.

"Kee-coo!" she said, proudly holding out one of the cookies her mother had baked for the picnic. Usually they weren't allowed to have dessert first. But Priscilla was something of a "cookie monster." It would have been impossible to bring a tray of cookies and Priscilla to the same place without giving her one.

Timothy said, "No, not kee-*coo*. You have it backwards again, Baby Girl. It's cookie. *Cook*-ee."

Priscilla nodded happily. "Kee-coo!"

"Arghh!" cried Timothy, pretending to

pull his hair out. "Why do I try?"

But seeing a baby with a cookie had suddenly reminded him of something.

The cousins had been so interested in the mysterious poncho-lady that they had almost forgotten about the baby elephant cookie jar.

Now the three cousins dragged Timothy's mother—laughing—to see the white elephant that *really was* a white elephant.

But when they got to the table, the baby elephant cookie jar was gone.

6

Stolen?

"*B*ut it was right here!" cried Timothy.

He pointed to the empty spot on the table where the cookie jar should have been.

Sarah-Jane said, "No one else could have bought it already. The auction isn't until after the picnic."

Titus said, "Maybe somebody else was looking at it and set it down in the wrong place."

Timothy knew his cousins were trying to make him feel better. But they sounded as puzzled—and worried—as he was.

Sarah-Jane had the idea of asking Mrs.

Foster if she had changed her mind about selling it.

But Mrs. Foster was just as puzzled as they were.

"No, I left the cookie jar right there. What in the world could have happened to it?

"It's no great loss, but I *do* hope nothing else is missing. I'd better go keep an eye on that gorgeous mirror! Excuse me."

And she hurried off. Timothy's parents stared after her. Then they turned to the cousins.

"Don't ask," said Titus.

"But it's true," said Sarah-Jane. "Mrs. Foster loved our mirror. And we loved her cookie jar."

And now the cookie jar was missing. The cousins decided to look around. Maybe someone *had* set the cookie jar down in the wrong place. It was time for another search. But this one wasn't for fun.

The cousins did a quick check of all the tables. Quick but careful. They looked everywhere. On the tables. Even under the tables. The baby elephant cookie jar was nowhere to be seen.

"Never mind, sweetie," said Timothy's mother when they reported back. "Why don't you pick out something else?"

"No!" cried Timothy. "I wanted you to have the cookie jar! Besides—it doesn't make sense."

Sarah-Jane and Titus nodded. They knew Timothy hated it when things didn't make sense. They felt the same way.

Timothy went on. "I mean, the cookie jar didn't just *walk* away. Does that mean somebody *stole* it?"

Sarah-Jane joined in, thinking things through. "But why steal it? The cookie jar was for sale. Why not just bid on it at the auction?"

Titus added, "And it wouldn't even cost that much. It's just a cookie jar. It's not like it was really valuable or anything."

Timothy's mother sighed. "I don't know what to tell you. I agree that it doesn't make sense for someone to take it. I hate to think anyone would. It would be like taking money from the church. Even if the jar wasn't worth much, it's still wrong. But let's not jump to conclusions. Why don't you talk to Pastor Parry about it?"

The cousins agreed that this was a good idea. And it gave them something to do. There was nothing worse than having a problem and not being able to do anything to solve it.

7

A Collector's Item

*T*imothy's parents went off to help with lunch. Timothy, Titus, and Sarah-Jane went to go look for Pastor Parry. But just as they did, they saw Pastor Parry heading in their direction. With him was Mr. Ramsey from the choir. Both men looked happy and excited.

"The most amazing thing!" said Pastor Parry to the cousins. "Mr. Ramsey tells me something quite valuable has shown up at our little swap meet. He's a collector, and he says a similar item recently sold for $350.00. He's offering the same amount. Isn't that wonderful? Now, we'd better set it aside so it doesn't get broken. And I need to talk to Mrs. Foster.

I'm sure she had no idea how valuable it was when she donated it."

The cousins gulped.

"You're talking about the baby elephant cookie jar, aren't you?" asked Titus.

"Yes," said Mr. Ramsey. "How did you know?"

"Because we wanted to buy it ourselves," replied Sarah-Jane. "Except we had no idea it could cost so much money!"

Timothy said, "But there's a problem. A BIG problem. The cookie jar is gone."

"What!?" cried Mr. Ramsey and Pastor Parry together. "What do you mean, *gone*?"

Timothy shook his head. "All I know is that we wanted to show it to my mom. But when we got to the table it was gone. We think somebody stole it."

"Maybe it was just misplaced," suggested Pastor Parry.

"We thought so, at first," Timothy said.

"But we can't find it," said Titus. "And we looked everywhere."

"Everywhere," said Sarah-Jane. "We even asked Mrs. Foster. She didn't know it was gone. And she wasn't the least bit worried when we told her. So I'm sure she doesn't know how much the cookie jar is worth."

"Oh, dear," sighed Pastor Parry. "I'd better have a quiet word with her. I'll also talk to the people in charge of the picnic. Maybe one of them set the cookie jar aside for some reason. Or maybe one of them saw something unusual. I really don't want to make a general announcement and ruin everyone's day unless I absolutely have to. Maybe we can track the cookie jar down ourselves."

Mr. Ramsey unhappily agreed that this was the right thing to do.

Pastor Parry smiled at the cousins. "We sure could use the T.C.D.C. right now."

"What's a 'teesy-deesy'?" asked Mr. Ramsey.

"It's letters," Timothy explained. "Capital T. Capital C. Capital D. Capital C. It stands for the Three Cousins Detective Club."

Mr. Ramsey looked a little doubtful. But Pastor Parry had seen firsthand how the cousins had solved mysteries before.

Pastor Parry and Mr. Ramsey went off to talk to Mrs. Foster. The cousins looked at one another. They had a mystery on their hands all right. And one thing was sure: This was no game.

8

Another Search

"**W**hat on earth are we going to do?" asked Timothy. "We already looked everywhere."

Titus said slowly, "Well, not exactly. We didn't look *everywhere*. We just looked all around the tables. That was when we thought someone misplaced the cookie jar by accident. But what if somebody hid the cookie jar on purpose?"

"You mean so they could get it later?" asked Sarah-Jane. "After the picnic when there weren't a lot of people around?"

"Exactly," said Titus.

"And maybe it's not even here anymore,"

said Sarah-Jane. "Maybe whoever stole it took it home already."

"Let's hope not!" said Timothy. "Let's hope whoever took it thought it would look suspicious to leave before the picnic even got started."

They all agreed that there was still a good chance the cookie jar was hidden somewhere around the church. And they knew they had to do their level-headed best to track it down.

Since they had already looked outside around the tables, they decided to try something different and look inside the church.

All the doors were locked except the side door, so there was a lot of coming and going through there. Just inside there was a landing and stairs leading down to the basement. From below they could hear voices and laughter and the clatter of pots and pans.

"What's downstairs?" asked Titus. "Just the kitchen?"

Timothy counted off on his fingers. "The kitchen. The washrooms. The social hall. The storage room. The Lost-and-Found closet. That's about it."

The cousins went downstairs, Timothy leading the way.

They peeked into the church kitchen. People scurried here and there, heating up food and making coffee.

"I don't think anyone could have hidden the cookie jar in the kitchen," Timothy said softly to his cousins. "There are just too many people around. It would have looked too suspicious if anyone had tried to hide anything."

They decided to skip the kitchen for now. They could always come back later.

They checked out the washrooms. Again, there were just too many people around.

Next they checked the social hall. With the picnic being held outside, the social hall was dim, cool, and quiet. The cousins tiptoed in and looked all through it. But there were hardly any hiding places. Not for something as big as a cookie jar. They checked the door to the storage room. Locked.

Timothy sighed. "Well, that's it for the inside. There's a lot of ground outside that we haven't covered yet. The bushes. The flower beds. The parking lot. Let's get started."

They were about to head upstairs when

Timothy turned back to a door tucked away under the stairs. A sign on the door said "Lost-and-Found."

Timothy said, "It wouldn't hurt to look in here. Besides, I should check on a pair of shoes Priscilla lost a couple of weeks ago."

Timothy pulled open the door. The Lost-and-Found closet was actually a tiny room. Just big enough for the three detective-cousins to step inside. The room was filled with all sorts of odds and ends.

They didn't find the cookie jar.

They didn't find Priscilla's shoes.

What they *did* find was a rain poncho and a big, floppy sun hat.

9

Lost-and-Found

*F*or a moment they just stared at the clothes as if they couldn't take in what they were seeing.

Then on impulse, Sarah-Jane grabbed the poncho and hat and put them on.

"How do I look?" she asked the boys.

"Ridiculous!" said Titus.

"Come on, S-J. Quit fooling around," said Timothy.

"Gentlemen. I am trying to make a point here."

"Which is?" asked Titus, super politely.

"Which is: That these clothes cover me up

from head to toe. Yes, they're too big for me. But these clothes are even big enough to hide a grown-up. Do you see what I'm getting at?"

The cousins often found that when they came up against something they didn't understand, it helped to talk things out.

Sarah-Jane continued. "When we saw that strange-looking lady by the tree, Tim said—"

Timothy jumped in. "I said: 'Why would you wear a rain poncho and a sun hat at the same time? Especially when you didn't need either one.' Answer: Because you wanted to be

all covered up. Because you didn't want anyone to see who you were. The poncho and the hat were a disguise!"

"That's what I think," said Sarah-Jane.

"So what are you saying?" asked Titus thoughtfully. "That somebody decided to wear a disguise and came looking in the Lost-and-Found for something to wear? Usually the Lost-and-Found just has little things—like scarves and stuff."

Timothy said, "These things weren't in the Lost-and-Found before. At least they weren't in here last Sunday when I came looking for Priscilla's shoes. I think somebody wore the disguise to church and then ditched the stuff in the closet when she didn't need it anymore."

"OK, I'll buy that," said Titus. "But why would anyone wear a disguise to a church picnic in the first place?"

Sarah-Jane raised her eyebrows and said what they were all thinking. "Because she was planning to steal a valuable cookie jar?"

Titus shrugged. "You guys? Is it just me? Or is this just about the most exasperating case we've ever had? I mean, every time we come up with an answer, we just get a harder question. OK. Let's say the poncho-lady came pre-pared with a disguise because she wanted to steal the cookie jar. How did she know the cookie jar would be here at the swap meet? And we're still stuck with the most important question of all: Where is the cookie jar *now*?"

All during this conversation with his cous-ins, Timothy had the strange feeling that his brain was trying to remember something. But what?

What?

He didn't know what.

Timothy sighed. "We don't even know *for sure* if the clothes have anything to do with the cookie jar at all."

"No, we don't," agreed Sarah-Jane. "But Pastor Parry said he was going to ask people if they had seen anything unusual. Well, we saw something unusual. There's no doubt about *that*!"

They bundled up the hat and poncho and went to find Pastor Parry. Sarah-Jane and Ti-tus said that Timothy should be the one to carry the things since it was his church.

As they scurried up the stairs and across the yard, Timothy still had the strange feeling of not being able to remember something. But he also had the feeling that it was coming closer.

"Something's missing," he said to his cousins. "There's something that should have been in the closet with the poncho and the hat. But it wasn't there."

"What? What?" cried Sarah-Jane and Titus together.

Timothy groaned. "That's the problem. I don't know what. I can't remember!"

Then suddenly—he did.

When he told his cousins, they stopped dead in their tracks and stared at him.

10

Something Unusual

When Pastor Parry saw the cousins rushing toward him, he came to meet them.

"You found it!" he exclaimed.

"Not exactly," gasped Timothy. "But we're close. Very close."

It was hard to calm down and explain. But if the cousins had learned anything about telling exciting things to grown-ups, it was that you had to take it slow. Otherwise, grown-ups would just make you take a deep breath and start over. And that was an even bigger waste of time than going slowly in the first place.

So Sarah-Jane started off with a deep

breath. "Pastor Parry, you said you were going to ask people if they had seen anything unusual."

He nodded. "I did ask the people on the picnic committee. But unfortunately, no one remembered seeing anything out of the ordinary. Maybe they were just too busy."

Sarah-Jane nodded back and took another deep breath. "Well, we saw something *very* unusual. And so did you."

"I did?" exclaimed Pastor Parry.

"Yes," said Titus. "Remember before most of the people got here? There was this lady? She was wearing these things here. Remember?"

Timothy held up the hat and the poncho and picked up on the story. "You started to come over to say hello to her. But she hurried away."

"Ah!" said Pastor Parry, remembering. "Now that you mention it, I *did* think that was odd. Most people get upset if the pastor *doesn't* say hello to them."

"We think she didn't want you to recognize her," said Timothy.

"Did you recognize her?" asked Titus.

46

"No," replied Pastor Parry, thinking back. "Of course, I couldn't see her face because of that big hat. But it didn't *seem* like anyone I knew. Do you know what I mean? I didn't think to myself, 'Oh, that's Mrs. So-and-So, wearing a big hat.' It was more like, 'I wonder who that could be?' I thought maybe she was a guest. But then I wondered why a guest would be here so early." He looked at the clothes. "But how do you come to have her things?"

"They were hanging in the Lost-and-Found," said Timothy.

Pastor Parry gave a low whistle. "That *is* unusual! You mean she just left them there? Does that mean she's long gone? Or does that mean she's still at the picnic—'disguised' as herself?"

"We don't know," said Timothy. "But what's really weird is what we *didn't* find. When we first saw her, she was carrying a beige tote bag. The tote bag was *not* in the Lost-and-Found."

Pastor Parry saw right away what they were getting at. He said, "Find the tote bag, and you'll find the cookie jar. Is that it?"

The cousins nodded. That was about the size of it.

11

A Red Leaf

*T*imothy said, "We started off thinking that the thief might have hidden the cookie jar somewhere in the church. But probably the poncho-lady thought that would make it too hard to get the cookie jar back at the end of the picnic. She didn't care if she couldn't get the clothes back. They're pretty old anyway. But it was different with the cookie jar. So then we thought that she would want to keep the cookie jar nearby. But it had to be in a place that didn't look suspicious."

Titus said, "A bag wouldn't look suspicious. Just about everyone has a bag of some kind. Kids have book bags. Even Priscilla has a diaper bag. The poncho-lady just had an ordinary beige tote bag."

Pastor Parry sighed. "That's where it gets sticky. There could be a lot of beige tote bags here today. And we can't just demand that people show us what's in them. That really would ruin everyone's day! And I don't know what I'm going to tell Mrs. Foster. She was thrilled to find out the jar was worth that much. She insisted the money should all go to the church building fund."

They were all quiet for a moment, wondering what to do next.

Pastor Parry said, "Tell you what. You kids have done such a fantastic job, I'm going to ask you to keep at it, all right?"

The cousins looked at one another. It was hard to keep from grinning. More detective work was always all right with them.

Pastor Parry said, "I'll try to keep an eye out for this tote bag. But right now I have to help with the picnic. So I want you three to keep looking around. Will you do that?"

"Yes, we will," said Timothy. "And don't worry. If the bag is still here, we'll find it."

Pastor Parry patted each of them on the back. "Great! When you find it, report back to me. I'll have a talk with the owner. I don't know what I'll say exactly. I'll have to play it by ear. The things they don't tell you in seminary!"

He started to walk off. Then he turned back. "Now tell me again what we're looking for. Just a plain beige tote bag?"

"No, not quite plain," said Timothy, thinking hard. He appealed to his cousins. "The tote bag had some sort of red design on it, remember? A red flower, maybe?"

"No," said Titus, suddenly remembering. "Not a flower—a leaf."

"A red leaf," said Sarah-Jane. "Like from a maple tree in the fall."

"A red maple leaf," repeated Pastor Parry. "Like the one on the Canadian flag? Is that what you mean?"

The cousins looked at one another. But this time they didn't feel like grinning. Yes, a Canadian maple leaf was exactly what they meant.

12

Coincidence?

*T*hey wanted to tell Pastor Parry what they were thinking. But before they could say anything, a group of people came over and began talking to him.

So the cousins went off and told themselves what they were thinking.

Sarah-Jane said, "The red maple leaf on the tote bag was just like the one on the Canadian flag. OK. So. A person could probably buy a tote bag like that as a souvenir in Canada. And we know Mrs. Foster's houseguest just got back from Canada." She frowned. "Of course, that doesn't prove she was the poncho-lady. Anybody can go to Canada and buy a tote bag. . . ."

Titus shook his head. "Is that too much of a coincidence? Because not just anybody knew Mrs. Foster was going to bring the cookie jar to the swap meet. Only Mrs. Foster's house-guest knew that. And she even tried to stop her by buying it herself, remember? She just made up the part about the white elephant being embarrassing."

Timothy said, "She tried to buy it for a few dollars. What a cheat."

Sarah-Jane said, "It would have been cheating if she had bid only a few dollars on it at the auction, too. But she knew guests couldn't bid on things their hosts had brought."

"And besides," added Titus. "What if someone came to the auction who *knew* the cookie jar was worth a lot? And what if that person was willing to pay full price? She couldn't get it cheap then. As it turned out, that's exactly what happened—with Mr. Ramsey. So Mrs. Foster's houseguest knew she really *had* to get her hands on the cookie jar before the sale."

Timothy said, "So she told Mrs. Foster she would come over later. But actually she came over early."

"Wearing an old rain poncho and a sun hat," said Sarah-Jane. "That was in case Mrs. Foster saw her. She didn't want to be recognized. Anyway, she just strolled over to the table when the coast was clear. And she just slipped the cookie jar into the tote bag. Even though we were watching her, we didn't see her do that. Maybe she used the rain poncho as a cover for what she was doing."

"But it wasn't all that easy for her," said Titus. "Because Pastor Parry started to come over to say hello. She couldn't let him see her up close. Because she knew Mrs. Foster would want to introduce them later. And what if Pastor Parry said, 'Weren't you the lady I saw earlier?' No, that would look too suspicious."

"So she had to get away," said Timothy. "Without looking suspicious. And the only place to go was the church. Maybe she wanted to look like she was going to help in the kitchen or use the washroom. She probably noticed the Lost-and-Found closet when she was down there. And she figured that was the perfect place to ditch the disguise. She could just hang around downstairs for a while—maybe in the social hall or the washroom. And then she could go find Mrs. Foster and pretend she just got here."

"Is she here now?" asked Titus, scanning the crowd.

But, of course, neither Titus nor Sarah-Jane could tell who was a visitor when they didn't know most of the people anyway.

But Timothy could. And he took a good look around.

"There she is!" he said, trying not to talk too loudly. "There's a lady with Mrs. Foster now. She's nobody I recognize from church. So that must be her."

The cousins could hardly stand still. It was so exciting, so satisfying, to figure things out like that. It took them a moment to realize that the lady wasn't carrying anything.

Where was the tote bag?

Where was the cookie jar?

13

Baby-Sitters and Detectives

The cousins felt like three balloons with all the air let out of them.

"Don't tell me she *hid* the tote bag somewhere," groaned Titus. "Oh, please—not another search. I feel like I've been hunting elephants my whole life."

Sarah-Jane shrugged helplessly. "What else can we do?"

"Let's get started then," said Timothy.

They were just about to go off on another search when Timothy's father came up to them. He was carrying Priscilla.

"There you are!" he said. "Where have you guys been?"

But before they could even begin to explain, he went on. "Listen, Priscilla's been asking for you constantly. 'Ware Timmy go? Ware Sayway-Zane? Ware Tidus?'"

The cousins couldn't help laughing. It sounded so funny to hear Timothy's father talking like Priscilla. Priscilla laughed, too—even though she had no idea what was so funny. And that made them laugh harder.

"So how about it, kids?" said Timothy's father. "Spend a little time with her, OK? After all, she's a cousin, too."

How could they say no to that? So they took Priscilla with them. Even though it meant they had to be baby-sitters *and* detectives. All at the same time.

Next to cookies and her blankie, Priscilla loved her stroller most of all. Sometimes she rode in it. Sometimes she insisted on pushing it herself. The cousins knew the stroller would keep her happy and quiet. And with Priscilla in the stroller, they could move around faster. So they walked her over to get it.

The stroller was propped up against a bench with a lot of other stuff that people had set down. Things like: Other strollers. Umbrellas. Jackets. Tote bags.

14

Exactly

*T*imothy scooped up Priscilla, and the four cousins practically flew to the bench.

Yes. There—hidden in plain sight among the other tote bags—was one with a telltale maple leaf.

While Sarah-Jane fumbled with Priscilla's stroller, Timothy and Titus fumbled with the tote bag.

"Hurry! *Hurry!*" Sarah-Jane muttered to the boys. To Priscilla she said, "Come over here, and be a good little baby detective. Sarah-Jane needs Priscilla to help block the boys while they're digging in a lady's tote bag." To the boys she said, "Is it there? Is it there?"

Titus said, "There's a sweater on top. And something underneath wrapped in newspapers."

"Maybe I can tear a little bit off," said Timothy. "And see if—yes!"

"Yes?" asked Sarah-Jane. "*Yes?*"

"Yes," said Timothy. "We found the jar!"

But how to get it to Pastor Parry without being seen?

"Quick," said Titus. "Put it in the pouch in back of Priscilla's stroller."

Sarah-Jane turned the stroller around, and the boys got the tote bag safely hidden.

They all let out a sigh of relief. Now all they had to do was put Priscilla in the stroller and whisk the whole thing off to Pastor Parry.

But Priscilla had other ideas. "Me me me me me me me me!"

"Oh, puh-leese!" groaned Titus. "Don't tell me that means what I think it means."

"It means she wants to push," said Timothy. "And take it from someone who knows. There's not a thing we can do about it."

So they made their way toward Pastor Parry, with Priscilla happily pushing her stroller. They were walking so slowly they thought they were going to topple over.

They walked right by Mrs. Foster and her friend. Fortunately, they were talking to some other people about Canada.

Not much farther.

Pastor Parry looked up and saw them coming. Even though they weren't rushing, he must have been able to guess something from their faces. "You found it!" he said, just as he had before.

And this time Timothy was able to say, "Exactly!"

15

Back to the Attic

"*H*ow is it possible that there could be two mirrors like that in the world?" exclaimed Timothy's father.

The swap meet was over. The cousins and Timothy's parents were back at home. They all sat around the kitchen table with the mirror in the middle. It wasn't the same mirror they had taken to the white elephant swap meet. But it was one just like it. Someone else had brought it and put it on the table at the last minute. But no one would admit bringing it. And Timothy's family had ended up with it because no one else would take it.

"Not even Mrs. Foster wanted two of them," said Titus.

"Poor Mrs. Foster," said Sarah-Jane. "It must be so awful to have a friend trick you like that. Even though her friend cried and said she was sorry."

They were all quiet, remembering how it had been. The cousins had just shown Pastor Parry the elephant in the tote bag. Then Mrs. Foster had come up, dragging her friend behind her. Her friend didn't want to make a fuss, Mrs. Foster had said. But her tote bag was missing. And wasn't that awful—on top of the missing cookie jar? And Pastor Parry had replied that what was even more awful was that the two things had been found in the same place.

That's when Mrs. Foster's friend had started crying. The cousins had gladly left Pastor Parry to sort that one out.

He must have done a good job, because Mrs. Foster had come over to thank them, and to tell them everything was going to be all right.

Timothy asked, "What did Mrs. Foster mean when she said her friend felt our church was the most loving place she'd ever been in? I mean, things didn't turn out so great for her. She got caught. And she didn't get to keep the cookie jar she wanted so much."

Timothy's father said, "Love doesn't mean that we get to do whatever we want. Love means that God wants what's best for us. And that's what we should want for other people— whatever's best for them. Stealing is not the best thing for anyone. Mrs. Foster's friend must have felt that the people at church really cared about her. Even when she didn't get her own way. She must have felt that she was valuable to them."

"She didn't feel like a white elephant," said Sarah-Jane.

"God doesn't have any white elephants," said Titus.

"Speaking of white elephants . . ." said Timothy's mother.

"Say no more," said Timothy, picking up the mirror.

And for the second time that day, he and his cousins went up to the attic.

The End